W9-CUE-008

Studio Fun International
An imprint of Printers Row Publishing Group
A division of Readerlink Distribution Services, LLC
10350 Barnes Canyon Road, Suite 100, San Diego, CA 92121
www.studiofun.com

Copyright © 2019 Disney Enterprises, Inc. All rights reserved.

No part of this publication may be reproduced, distributed, or transmitted in any form or by any means, including photocopying, recording, or other electronic or mechanical methods, without the prior written permission of the publisher, except in the case of brief quotations embodied in critical reviews and certain other noncommercial uses permitted by copyright law.

Printers Row Publishing Group is a division of Readerlink Distribution Services, LLC.
Studio Fun International is a registered trademark of Readerlink Distribution Services, LLC.

All notations of errors or omissions should be addressed to Studio Fun International,
Editorial Department, at the above address.

ISBN: 978-0-7944-4572-0
Manufactured, printed, and assembled in Dongguan, China.
First printing, July 2019. RRD/07/19
23 22 21 20 19   1 2 3 4 5

Disney

Lady and the TRAMP

studio **fun**
INTERNATIONAL

"Merry Christmas, Darling!" said Jim Dear as he handed his wife a pink striped box. Inside was a little brown puppy.

Darling took one look at the puppy and decided to call her Lady.

Lady was happy in her new home. She slept in the same room with Jim Dear and Darling.
She romped in the yard and kept watch over the house.

When Lady was older, Jim Dear and Darling gave her a collar with a name tag. Lady proudly showed her collar to her friends Jock and Trusty.

"She's a full-grown lady," said Jock.

Tramp was another dog who was sometimes in the neighborhood. He didn't have a warm home and family. He liked to wander the streets, looking for scraps and helping his friends escape from the dogcatcher.

Tramp overheard Jock and Trusty telling Lady that Jim Dear and Darling were expecting a baby.

"What's a baby?" Lady asked.

"A home-wrecker, that's what," said Tramp. Lady's happy life was about to change.

One rainy April day, the baby came. Jim Dear and Darling were thrilled with their new little boy. Lady liked the baby, too.

Jim Dear and Darling decided to take a trip. Aunt Sarah came to look after the baby. Her two cats came, too. Aunt Sarah was not very nice to Lady.

Her two cats were not very nice, either. They made a mess of the house and pretended that Lady caused the trouble. "Oh, that wicked animal!" said Aunt Sarah.

Aunt Sarah took Lady straight to the pet store.
"I want a good, strong muzzle," Aunt Sarah said.
The muzzle scared Lady. She jumped off the counter and ran
out the door.

She ran and ran. Soon some big, mean dogs started to chase after her. Lady was scared. Luckily, Tramp heard all the barking and raced to Lady's rescue.

"Oh, poor kid," said Tramp, looking at Lady's muzzle. "We've gotta get this thing off. Come on."

Tramp took Lady to the zoo. Maybe one of the animals could help Lady.

The apes, the alligator, and the hyena were no help at all. Then Lady and Tramp found the beaver. He loved to chew and soon bit right through the muzzle strap.

"It's off!" Lady said with relief.

The beaver was happy, too. He could use the muzzle as a handy-dandy log puller.

Then Tramp took Lady to supper at Tony's Restaurant. Tramp's friend Tony liked Lady and fed the pair his specialty—spaghetti with meatballs!

Tramp and Lady accidentally ate the same spaghetti noodle.
Next thing they knew, they were kissing! Lady and Tramp were
falling in love.

The happy pair walked to the top of a hill. They gazed up at the full moon that shone over their town. It was such a beautiful night.

The next morning, on the way home, Tramp and Lady passed
a chicken coop.
"Ever chased chickens?" Tramp asked. He couldn't resist.
Lady did not like the idea, but she followed him anyway.

The chickens ran around the yard squawking and squealing. "Hey, what's going on in there?" the farmer called.

Lady and Tramp ran away as fast as they could. But Tramp soon discovered that Lady wasn't behind him. She had run into the dogcatcher and was taken to the dog pound!

Lady was scared to be at the dog pound. But soon the dogcatcher came for her. Reading her collar, he knew where to take her.

"You're too nice a girl to be in this place," he said, and returned Lady to Aunt Sarah.

At home, Aunt Sarah chained Lady to the doghouse. Lady was so sad, even Jock and Trusty could not cheer her up.

Then Tramp arrived. Lady was angry with him. She thought Tramp had only looked out for himself and had let her get caught by the dogcatcher.

He tried to explain. "I thought you were right behind me, honest," he said.

"Goodbye. And take this with you," Lady said, returning the bone Tramp had brought for her.

That night, Lady saw a rat creeping into the baby's room.
She couldn't chase it because of the chain. She could only bark.
"Stop that!" Aunt Sarah called. "Hush."
But Tramp heard and rushed back to Lady.

"What is it?" Tramp asked.

"A rat in the baby's room," Lady replied.

Tramp ran into the house and found the rat. He had to catch that rat before it hurt the baby.

Meanwhile, Lady was barking with all her
might and pulling on the heavy chain. At
last the chain broke free from the doghouse.
Lady ran inside to help Tramp.

Tramp chased the rat under the baby's bassinet and accidentally knocked it over. The baby started to cry. But Lady was happy because the baby was safe—Tramp had finally caught the rat.

Aunt Sarah was not happy. The baby's crying woke her, and she found Lady and Tramp in his room. She thought they were hurting the baby. She called the dogcatcher to come for Tramp.

The dogcatcher soon arrived.

Just then, Jim Dear and Darling came home. Lady tried to explain what had happened. She lifted the curtain to show that Tramp had caught the rat and saved the baby.

Jock and Trusty had a plan to stop the dogcatcher's wagon. They barked loudly, scaring the horses. The wagon crashed, and Tramp was safe. Jim Dear and Lady soon arrived to bring him home.

The next Christmas Eve, Jock and Trusty came by to see Lady, Tramp—and their four new puppies.

"They've got their mother's eyes," said Trusty.

"There's a bit of their father in them, too," said Jock.

Everyone was happy that Tramp
had become part of the family.